Hit a Grand Slam

By Alex Rodriguez

with Greg Brown

Illustrations by Doug Keith

I dedicate this book to my mother, who taught me true family values through her daily examples of love, courage, dedication, and sacrifice while always holding on to dreams of a better tomorrow. My heartfelt thank you goes to my family—especially Leoni, Mercedes, Susy, Joseph, and Yuri—for their lifelong unconditional support. Additionally, I'd like to thank the Arteaga family, Christina, Rich, and Eddy, for their guidance and friendship. I'd also like to thank Scott Boras for his invaluable counsel.

The Boys and Girls Club of Miami was always there when I was in need. I will continue my work to support the Boys and Girls Clubs of America with royalties received from the publication of this book.

—Alex

Alex can be found on the Internet at www.A-Rod.com.

Greg Brown has been involved in sports for thirty years as an athlete and award-winning sportswriter. Brown started his Positively For Kids series after being unable to find sports books for his own children that taught life lessons. He is the co-author of *Kristi Yamaguchi: Always Dream; John Elway: Comeback Kid; Scottie Pippen: Reach Higher; Dan Marino: First and Goal; Kerri Strug: Heart of Gold; Mo Vaughn: Follow Your Dreams; Sheryl Swoopes: Bounce Back; Steve Young: Forever Young; Bonnie Blair: A Winning Edge; Cal Ripken Jr.: Count Me In; Troy Aikman: Things Change; Kirby Puckett: Be the Best You Can Be;* and *Edgar Martinez: Patience Pays.* Brown regularly speaks at schools and can be reached at greg@PositivelyForKids.com. He lives in Bothell, Washington, with his wife, Stacy, and two children, Lauren and Benji.

Doug Keith provided the illustrations for the best-selling children's book *Things Change* by Troy Aikman, *Heart of Gold* by Kerri Strug, *Count Me In* by Cal Ripken Jr, *A Winning Edge* by Bonnie Blair, *Bounce Back* by Sheryl Swoopes, *Forever Young* by Steve Young, *Reach Higher* by Scottie Pippen, *Comeback Kid* by John Elway, and *Always Dream* by Kristi Yamaguchi. His illustrations have appeared in national magazines such as *Sports Illustrated for Kids*, greeting cards, and books. Keith can be reached at his internet address: atozdk@aol.com.

All photos courtesy of Alex Rodriguez and family unless otherwise noted.

Copyright © 1998 by Alex Rodriguez and Greg Brown

Published by Taylor Publishing Company
1550 West Mockingbird Lane
Dallas, Texas 75235

Designed by Steve Willgren

Library of Congress Cataloging-in-Publication Data
Rodriguez, Alex, 1975–
    Hit a grand slam / by Alex Rodriguez with Greg Brown ; illustrations by Doug Keith.
        p.   cm.
    Summary: The superstar shortstop for the Seattle Mariners discusses how education, hard work, and doing the right thing helped him become a Major League All-Star and the American League's leading hitter in 1996.
        1. Rodriguez, Alex, 1975–   —Juvenile literature. 2. Baseball players—United States—Biography—Juvenile literature.
    [1. Rodriguez, Alex, 1975–   . 2. Baseball players. 3. Dominican Americans—Biography.] I. Brown, Greg.
    II. Keith, Doug, ill. III. Title.
    GV865.R62A3   1998
    796.357'092—dc21
    [B]   98-21336
                                                                        CIP
                                                                        AC

Printed in the United States of America
10 9 8 7 6 5 4 3 2 1

Alex at age 10

Tom Dipace

Hi! I'm Alex Rodriguez. People in Seattle sometimes call me A-Rod.

After two full seasons in the Major Leagues as the shortstop for the Seattle Mariners, I still have much to learn about both baseball and life.

Even though I'm young, I've written this book to share with you some of my experiences and the truths I've picked up along the way.

When I speak at elementary schools, I talk about hitting a grand slam for education. I hope all who read this book will realize that everyone, young and old, can hit a grand slam.

Both pictures capture memories of my first grand slam, April 18, 1996, in Seattle's Kingdome.

I don't mean everyone can hit a home run with the bases loaded. Many players never hit a grand slam in their entire careers.

Hitting a home run is never easy. When you swing for a homer, you usually strike out. Only a sweet, smooth swing produces a home run.

So far, I've hit a home run about every 22 times at bat on average.

Grand slams are much rarer. A grand slam is one of the most thrilling plays in baseball. I've been fortunate to hit three of them in four seasons in the big leagues, about one

in every 461 plate appearances.

My first three were all in Seattle's Kingdome during my first full season in the majors in 1996.

The type of grand slam I'd like to talk to you about might not seem as exciting, but it's something anyone can do.

When I talk with kids, I speak about hitting four different bases: reading, math, physical fitness, and citizenship.

When someone succeeds in these four areas, in my book they've hit a grand slam.

Reading is the cornerstone of education. Trying to learn without reading is like hitting without a bat. And just like sports, the only way to improve is to practice.

Just as important is understanding basic math. No matter how much money you make, you need to know how to manage what money you have.

While you train your mind, don't forget to exercise your body. Physical fitness is essential.

Finally, a sharp mind and healthy body do not mean much if you can't get along with others. That's why citizenship is so important.

Whenever I speak about these issues, I also tell about the events that have shaped me into the person I am today. That's what this book is all about—my early life stories.

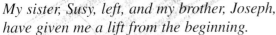
My sister, Susy, left, and my brother, Joseph, have given me a lift from the beginning.

Born July 27, 1975, in New York City, I'm told I was far from a perfect child.

My parents owned a shoe store in Manhattan, and we lived behind it. You could say my father, Victor, spoiled me. He babysat me during the day and ran the shoe store, while my mother, Lourdes, left at 4:00 in the morning to work on an assembly line at General Motors.

Dad had played amateur baseball in the Dominican Republic, so he put a bat in my hands early.

I remember carrying around a huge plastic red bat. I'd swat at everything within reach, often breaking things.

I also recall throwing a small rubber ball against the hallway wall for hours.

Cousins join me (wearing blue shirt) in my parents' shoe store in New York.

My favorite thing of all, however, was playing pinball.

Practically from when I started talking, I'd ask daily for "dollar pizza."

That meant I wanted four quarters and someone to walk me to the nearby pizza parlor so I could play the pinball machine. Sometimes I'd demand it. I'd beg my father. I'd tug on the clothes of my sister or brother with my hand out, shouting, "DOLLAR PIZZA!"

If I didn't get my way, I'd flop onto the floor and burst into a screaming, kicking, temper tantrum.

My family usually gave in. I remember New York as my perfect world.

My first bike.

Mom and me.

*Mom, Dad, and me in
our new home.*

*The front
door of our
house.*

My parents had different ideas about paradise.

Their dream was to make enough money in New York so they could return to their homeland in the Dominican Republic, an island between Cuba and Puerto Rico, and live an upper-class life.

After I turned four, they had saved enough money to return home. We moved to the Dominican Republic. My parents bought a four-bedroom dream home in a safe neighborhood about a block from the ocean in the capital city of Santo Domingo. We even had a live-in maid.

For several years, we lived the good life.

My first day of kindergarten.

My aunt and grandmother at my birthday party.

My aunts, uncles, and grand-parents lived nearby, and we all got together for celebrations, including my birthdays.

When I reached school age, I walked out our door eager to learn. I quickly found out kindergarten would be tougher than I thought.

Actually, getting to school was the toughest part. Every day during my first year of school, the bumpy bus ride made me dizzy.

Within days I had a routine. A bus attendant would give me a bag as I boarded, and every day I'd throw up into the paper bag at my bus seat.

No matter how sick I felt from the bus, I was always ready to play sports after school with neighborhood friends. We'd play in the street or at the huge park across from my house.

But the park grass sometimes grew over our heads, as you can see in this picture. Once a month it would be cut. Then, for a dozen days, we'd play marathon baseball games.

Always the youngest kid, I played second base because my arm wasn't strong enough to throw from shortstop to first base. We played against other neighborhoods, and those games were some of the most intense I've been in.

Whatever game I played, I couldn't handle losing. If I lost, I would go home crying angry tears. The whole night I would think of ways we could win the next day.

When the grass grew too high, sometimes we'd play "hot box," which is like being in a baseball run-down or "pickle."

But my favorite street game was what we called "Platicka." We took old car license plates and bent them to stand as two targets 90 feet apart. Two pitchers played against two hitters. The pitchers tried to knock down the plates with a rubber ball. Hitters protected the plate by swinging at the pitched ball with a stick. If you hit it, then you'd run and switch bases with your teammate to score. After three outs, hitters and pitchers traded places.

Just down the street at the edge of the park were outdoor basketball courts. My brother used to take me there. I loved shooting hoops, and I still do.

One afternoon, when I was seven, I went to the court by myself. A 20-year-old guy stood shooting baskets alone.

"Don't touch the ball," he said as I went for the loose ball.

A few minutes later the ball rolled near me again. I grabbed it and passed it to him.

"Don't touch the ball again!" he shouted.

Again, the ball bounced toward me. This time I put up a shot.

The guy rushed toward me with wild eyes. I started to run, but he was too fast. When he got near, the bully delivered a vicious kick to my backside, lifting me off my feet.

The coward ran off, and I limped home. The whole neighborhood searched but never found him. Fortunately, I escaped with bruises from my only street fight.

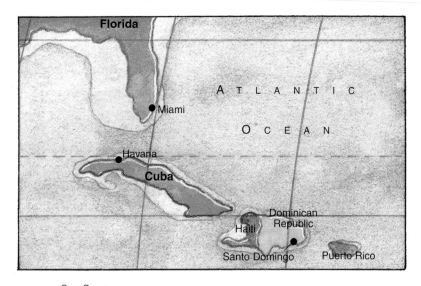

Greg Brown

Our rental house in Miami.

Sometimes parents get kicked down by life, which can be a bully, too. It happened to my parents when I was eight.

A poor economy forced them to sell their dream home and move to Miami after losing their business investment in a Dominican Republic pharmacy store.

My parents told me we'd move back in a few months, but we never did. I took it in stride.

Playing sports became my dream. I turned into a baseball freak. If I saw a favorite player using a black bat, I'd spend hours using shoe polish and a felt-tip pen to turn mine black, too.

Without question, the player I looked up to the most was Baltimore shortstop Cal Ripken, Jr. I wanted to play shortstop.

Mostly, though, I just wanted to play.

My transition from speaking all Spanish in the Dominican Republic to English-based fourth grade proved rocky.

I struggled in school for a couple of years as I became bilingual.

Fortunately, I was fluent in the universal language of sports.

Soon after we moved, I learned that a team practiced at our Everglades Elementary after school.

I went to practice every day for a month. I'd sit at the base of a tree and watch, thinking I'd give anything to play.

One day the team's catcher didn't show up. The coach, Juan Diego Arteaga, called to me: "Hey kid, do you want to play?"

"What do you want me to do?" I answered.

"Have you ever caught before?"

"Sure, sure. I'm a good catcher," I said, even though I had never caught before.

The team scrimmaged, and I caught a great game, even though I was a couple of years younger than most.

Mr. Arteaga introduced me to his son, J.D., who was on the team, and then drove me home. We lived only two blocks from each other.

Thanks to baseball, that day I met my best friend and a kind man who would become a second father to me.

A few weeks later, my father announced to the family that he needed to leave and work in New York for a short time.

He promised to return. When you're young, you believe your dad. I knew he'd come back as surely as the sun would rise on the Sunshine State. He had been a great dad. He played catch with me. He taught me math. He loved me.

"Dad's coming back, you'll see," I'd say defiantly to my sister.

But each passing week dug deeper a grave of pain. Finally, my hope dried up and died. I gave up.

Dad never came back.

I thirsted for Dad for so long. I have not seen him since. I can count on one hand the times I've talked to my father by phone since he left. I still don't understand how a parent could abandon a family.

Perhaps one day I'll reunite with him face to face. Maybe then I'll understand. Or maybe I never will. Whatever his true reasons for leaving and not staying in touch, I can forgive him. I have to let go of that anger to move forward. The problem is, I can't forget what he did.

Tragically, families split up every day. The fact that it happens to others didn't help me. And I don't agree if someone says that because it happened to Alex Rodriguez it will be easier for today's children who lose parents.

Pain is pain. That's number one. Everyone's situation is different. I was fortunate to have a team of people to guide me.

No matter what, we all need support—family members, friends, and other adults. Don't be afraid to talk with someone if you are hurting inside. Here are some reference numbers of people who can help:

Childhelp USA 1.800.4.A.CHILD

National Youth Crisis Center 1.800.HIT.HOME

Raising Today's Teens 1.800.475.TALK

Our family teetered financially for six months after Dad left. Mom worked at two restaurants as a waitress and did other odd jobs to pay our rent and keep food on the table.

Mom deserves the Oscar for acting as if we had plenty of money. Mom always has been the driving force in our family. Her perseverance and inner strength kept us together.

She was willing to do whatever it took to make our lives better. Mom did it with courage, never fearing the unknown, and optimism.

"Things will work out, you'll see," she'd say.

The highlight of my day was when Mom came home in the evening. She'd dump her restaurant tips on the floor, and I would count the money.

"Mom, you made $40. You had a good night," I'd say with delight.

My nights weren't always so great. Darkness and silence were my fears. To escape, I slept in my Mom's half-empty bed many nights for the next few years.

Whenever I see Mom, I always greet her with a kiss and kiss her good-bye. It's my way of showing her respect and gratitude for all the things she's done for me.

Tom Dipace

Realizing my tender emotions, Mom, Susy, Joe, and relatives blanketed me with attention and love. They couldn't replace my father, but they helped fill the hole.

Soon I found I had a team of special people on my side.

Mr. Arteaga introduced me to the Boys and Girls Clubs of Miami, which had the area's best baseball teams, and a man there who would become another father-figure—Eddy Rodriguez (no relation).

Eddy still runs programs and helps coach baseball, just as he did when I was there. The Boys and Girls Clubs played a crucial role by giving me something to do after school, instead of sitting alone at home and feeling sorry for myself.

Mr. Arteaga and Eddy guided me and gave me their most precious gift—time. Mr. Arteaga often drove J.D. and me to and from the Boys Club and to all the games. He'd check up on me and make sure I never went home to an empty house.

Greg Brown

Tom Dipace

Eddy played minor-league baseball and filled my head with his stories. He told of the great players he coached at the Boys Club: Jose Canseco, Rafael Palmeiro, Danny Tartabull, and Alex Fernandez. Hearing those stories helped me see myself as a pro player.

Even though my family couldn't afford the baseball registration fee, Mr. Arteaga worked it out so I could play. And whenever J.D. needed baseball gear, his father bought two and gave one to me.

As a skinny, shy kid, I proved myself by winning the league batting title.

Two things stand out in my memory of that first season in Florida.

With Mom, Susy, and Joe working hard to pay bills, seldom were they able to watch me play.

I remember staring as teammates munched on snacks and guzzled pops their parents brought between double-headers.

It hurt a little inside not having those treats. But I knew Mom was doing the best she could. Our family never went hungry, and we always had a home.

I felt like an underdog, but I never let my situation keep me down. I generally had a smile on my face.

J.D. and me with our game faces on.

I must have been beaming the first game my family did see. Naturally, I wanted to play well and show off a bit.

Going into my last at-bat of the game I was hitless in three tries.

I'm the type who doesn't want to talk to anyone when I'm not playing well. I was nervous anyway, because I thought if I didn't get a hit maybe my family wouldn't come again.

I walked to the plate and my whole family was waving and yelling, "Allllex! Allllex! We're over here."

I refused to look at them. Determined to get a hit no matter what, I struck out swinging at a pitch over my head.

A few years later, I made another embarrassing play. Our tournament team needed one more win to advance to the state championships. The opponents had a runner on second with two outs. Everyone thought we had won when a grounder came my way at shortstop. The ball bounced right through my legs, and we lost.

During my time at the Boys Club, our teams won two national titles and three city championships.

Eddy is the best practice coach I ever had. Sometimes we'd practice twice a day in the summer. Eddy showed us that practice is a price of success.

What really increased our skills were month-long road trips. We'd take off in vans with Mr. Arteaga and other parents and travel all over the country.

Some of our best games weren't played on the field, though. We entertained ourselves between games by playing "sock ball" in our hotel rooms.

The pitcher would stand in the bathroom and throw a balled-up sock. We'd hit with an open hand. No matter how hard we tried not to, we'd usually knock over a lamp or break something.

That's about the most trouble we caused. Coaches and parents impressed upon us that our actions were a reflection of our families, our neighborhood, and the Boys and Girls Clubs. We didn't want to let everyone down by doing something stupid.

Thinking of girls can make guys do some stupid things. I remember walking around an unfamiliar neighborhood with J.D. for four hours trying to find the home of a girl I liked in sixth grade.

She was my first date. We went to the movies and held hands. The excitement of that night vanished the next day when she dumped me.

We can laugh about it now, and we're still friends.

This picture of Mom and me was taken in our living room before my first junior high dance. As you can see, even then I took pride in looking sharp.

My rule of thumb is you can never be overdressed.

When you look like a slob, generally, you get treated like a slob. As you get older, you'll find people will respect you more if you're well dressed. It can open all kinds of doors. Then it's all up to you.

So you want to break up...

For various reasons, I attended four different schools in four years. I went to Kendall Academy in seventh grade and played on the varsity baseball team. There I am above in the front row on the far left. I was a kid playing with young men in high school. J.D.'s on the right end and the guy kneeling next to him is James Colzie, another long-time friend.

That summer, I burned out on baseball and talked about quitting the sport. I thought about focusing on basketball instead. Mom called a family meeting, and we talked about my options. She convinced me to "give baseball one more season."

Playing on teams with older guys never intimidated me. I always felt it helped me improve faster. Although my teammates were older, I still hung out with kids my own age.

I went to a different school in eighth grade and then to Christopher Columbus Catholic High in ninth grade. As a freshman, I played varsity basketball and found success on the court. Again, I thought my future might be in basketball, especially when the Columbus baseball coach decided I would play backup shortstop. He said, "We have a shortstop the next two years. Maybe as a senior you'll get an opportunity to play."

Christopher Columbus Catholic High School

Looking back, it's easy for people to criticize him. But I've never said anything bad about him. I honestly feel that at that time he had a better shortstop than me.

It all worked out for the best. Being the backup motivated me to work harder and forced me to look elsewhere. J.D., who decided on baseball power Westminster Christian High instead of Columbus, and his father convinced me to transfer to Westminster for my sophomore season.

Christopher Columbus Catholic High School

Christopher Columbus Catholic High School

*Jordan sticks out his tongue when he plays.
I bite my lips.*

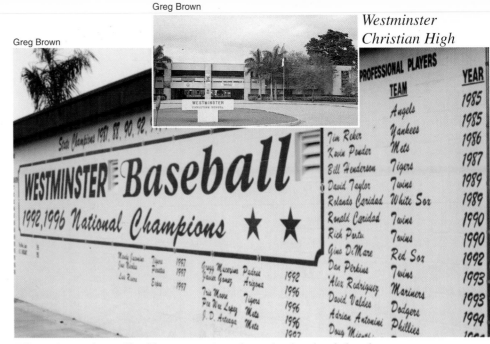

Westminster's wall of honor, painted on the back of the dugout.

The $5,000-a-year tuition to attend Westminster seemed an unpassable roadblock. My family couldn't afford it.

I applied for and received financial aid. It humbled me, but I wasn't ashamed to accept the help. We all need help at times.

Westminster was about 30 minutes away from my house by car, so I'd leave at 6:30 A.M. and often wouldn't get home until 8:00 P.M.

Mom gave me $20 a day for food and spending money. I didn't realize until later how Mom sacrificed her needs to give me that money every day.

I took school seriously. I made the honor roll and stayed out of trouble, playing all three major sports.

I earned the starting shortstop job my sophomore season, but produced my lowest-ever batting average—.256.

I had just gone through a growth spurt and still wasn't used to my lanky frame. I still didn't have a strong throwing arm and could barely bench-press 100 pounds.

I vowed to get stronger. I remem-ber lifting in the weight room after the season. Coach Rich Hofman, Westminster's long-time baseball coach who helped 75 former players advance to college baseball, 29 to professional ball, sat by me.

"Well, 10th grade you had an OK year. Next year everyone will get to know you, and in 12th grade you'll be the No. 1 pick in the country. Work hard this year!"

Coach Hofman instilled so much confidence in me that day. I'll never forget it. He raised the stakes. I felt I couldn't let him down.

Alex earned All-State football honors two years as quarterback and set several school passing records. He wore No. 13 because it is Dan Marino's number.

Mr. Arteaga

The ripples of his kindness
reached many people.
He treated me as a son,
and I miss him as a father.

Another factor contributing to my slow start as a sophomore was a heavy heart.

During a football game that fall, I lost a father a second time.

Someone ran into our halftime locker room and shouted, "A man collapsed in the stands!"

Once we heard it was Mr. Arteaga, J.D. started running. I followed. "J.D., he'll be all right."

Mr. Arteaga had a history of heart problems. Officials canceled the game while medics worked on him. A helicopter landed on the field and airlifted J.D.'s dad to the hospital.

I couldn't handle any of it. I couldn't even look at Mr. Arteaga on the ground. I refused to go to the hospital. Later that day word came that Mr. Arteaga had died.

I felt someone had torn my heart out and smashed it.

I know Mr. Arteaga and his family have forgiven me for not showing up at the hospital. I'm not sure I've forgiven myself.

At the time, I couldn't say good-bye. So now, before every baseball game I play, I silently say hello to Mr. Arteaga in my heart.

I don't know why Mr. Arteaga died then. I do believe God has a plan and things happen for a reason. Sometimes we just can't understand it.

J.D. and I grew closer, as brothers. We shared each other's loss, although we really didn't talk about it much. We gave each other strength.

My physical strength improved by my junior year. I could bench-press 310 pounds and hit the ball 400 feet. Coach Hofman was right. People did get to know me—and our whole team. That's because we finished No. 1 in the country in two polls—a first in school history—with a 32-2 record.

Alex earned All-America honors as a junior with a .477 batting average, 42 stolen bases, 6 home runs, and 52 runs scored.

J.D. and I show off our national championship rings. I decided to use a wood bat in high school instead of the more powerful aluminum so I'd be ready for pro baseball, which doesn't allow metal bats.

26

Greg Brown

"Hit it in the pool, Alex"

Westminster High has an outdoor pool just beyond the left-field fence. A teammate's father, Mr. Perez, used to yell for me to hit a home run into the pool when I batted. That embarrassed me so much. I hit 17 home runs in high school and had my share of "pool shots."

That summer I played on the USA junior national team. While playing in Mexico, I heard the news that Hurricane Andrew had slammed 190-mile-per-hour winds into Miami, killing 32 people.

I frantically called home, but I couldn't get through for three agonizing days.

Once I did, it was such a relief to hear that my family and everyone I knew made it through unscathed. Our school wasn't so lucky. Damage from Andrew delayed school six weeks. Some of us wondered if we'd have a senior sports year at all. But Andrew also gave us a gift of perspective on life.

We finally started the football season. After earning the starting quarterback job my junior year and leading our team to a 9-1 record, there were tall expectations on me as a senior. Many major colleges thought of me as a quarterback recruit.

Unfortunately, we didn't have a strong football team my senior season. I spent much of it running for my life on offense.

My prospects for any sport were in doubt for a few days that fall after I hurt my throwing wrist while tackling on a kickoff. Everyone held their breath for the medical report. I was scared until we found out it was just a hairline fracture.

I recovered quickly and chose to skip basketball to focus on baseball. J.D. and I signed letters of intent to play baseball at the University of Miami before our final season together started.

We had many talented baseball players my senior season. Everyone expected us to defend our national championship.

We almost won back-to-back titles, but a loss in the state quarterfinals ended the season. I had one error in that 11-inning 4–3 loss. I redeemed myself with a 2-run homer in the 7th to force extra innings.

Although we didn't repeat, I was proud of how the team handled all the publicity and pressure.

Throughout my senior season and into summer the stress on me intensified as I indeed became the No. 1 prospect in the country.

Tom Dipace

Miami Herald

Alex hit safely in half his at-bats as a senior, with a .505 average. He belted 9 home runs. As the leadoff batter, he reached base safely 21 consecutive times during a stretch early in the season. He stole 90 bases in 94 tries during his high school career.

For example, 68 scouts watched our season opener. I went 3-for-4 with a home run. Seventy-two showed up for our second game. Newspaper headlines called me Superman. It was a crazy time. Everyone wanted a piece of me.

Susy returned home from college to help answer 30–40 phone calls a night from scouts, college coaches, and sports agents.

The most important call came on draft day, when the Seattle Mariners made me the overall No. 1 pick. Family and friends all celebrated with me.

I had my worries about the Mariners. All I knew was they had a long tradition of losing seasons. The past 10 years my teams had won eight championships. All I knew was winning. But it turned out to be the best place to start my career.

Negotiations with the M's dragged on. Meanwhile, I became the first high school player invited to try out for the USA National Team.

The experience became my first taste of the business side of baseball. A cardmaker sponsored the team and expected all players to be in a card set. But that would have cost me at least $500,000 in lost income with another baseball card company.

I told team officials I couldn't agree to the card deal. I got cut.

Later that summer, I played at the U.S. Sports Festival in San Antonio with the junior national team. While in our dugout, a wildly thrown warm-up ball struck me in the cheek, knocking me out cold.

When I awoke, I started panicking as everyone who looked at my face

AP/Wide World Photos

turned away. I spent several nights in the local hospital with a caved-in face. Just as a car dent can be popped back flat, doctors drilled a hole above my ear and inserted a rod that popped my cheekbone back to normal.

Again, perspective slapped me in the face. If the ball had hit an inch higher, I could have died. An inch to the side, and I might have lost an eye. I didn't touch a baseball for 2½ months.

My family celebrates my signing with the Mariners.

Talks with the Mariners went down to the wire. The day before I was supposed to start classes at the University of Miami, we reached an agreement on my first baseball contract.

My first spring training opened my eyes to how hard pro athletes work. The posted time for practice was ten o'clock in the morning. Every day for a month I showed up at 9:30, figuring being early would show my dedication. One day I decided to arrive at 7:00 A.M. I walked in and saw a few guys already in the clubhouse.

I turned the corner into the weight room and saw second baseman Joey Cora pumping iron. I then went to the batting cage and found two-time batting champion Edgar Martinez hitting off a batting tee into a net.

"Edgar, what are you doing here so early?"

"I have to hit. I have to work!"

Most guys would go home at about two o'clock in the afternoon. One day I forgot my pager. I returned to the clubhouse and found Edgar in the batting cage at 6:00 P.M.

Those veterans showed me that success in anything begins with dedication and hard work.

I met NBA coach Pat Riley recently, and he told me a key to success is enjoying your sweat. That means you have to find joy in practice and working out to reach your highest athletic potential.

My first spring training I learned much by watching the veteran players.

The first picture day for baseball cards is a proud day for any rookie.

I started my first season at the bottom of the Mariners' minor leagues with Wisconsin's Class A Appleton Foxes. Players tell horror stories about the minor leagues, but playing in Appleton gave me cherished memories.

The town embraced me with a welcoming hug.

Within two months, I moved up to Class AA at Jacksonville. Three weeks later, I got the call to join the big-league team, that week playing in Boston.

I stayed up late calling family, friends, and old coaches—"I'm going to the show!"

At 18, I became the youngest Major League player in a decade. The lights, reporters, and crowds were unbelievable.

I remember preparing for my first at-bat in the on-deck circle. Ken Griffey, Jr. walked by and said: "It's showtime."

My body felt jittery, and my knees buckled. I could barely stand. I went hitless in three tries that first night, but I had a solid fielding night.

The next night I broke out with two hits. Still, I was nervous for days. I didn't want to make a mistake. I arrived early at the ballpark, hoping not to be noticed.

Jacksonville Suns

Tom Dipace

Appleton Baseball Club

Tacoma Rainiers

After 26 days, the Mariners sent me down to their Class AAA team in Calgary, Canada. That gave me the rare glimpse of playing in all four pro levels in one season.

I started the 1995 season with the Tacoma Rainiers, the M's new Class AAA affiliate. The 31-mile trip between Tacoma and Seattle became all too familiar. I was called up to Seattle on May 6th and stayed 21 days, enduring the rookie razzing.

The Mariners have a special rookie tradition for the team's first series in Kansas City. When I got out of the shower after the last game, all my clothes were gone. Instead, I had to sign 30 autographs while wearing a silver dress and balancing in high-heeled shoes. If that wasn't bad enough, I had to wear them on the flight home and listen to all the teasing jokes. I laughed along with them.

Much of that season was no laughing matter to me. I became a human yo-yo going between Tacoma and Seattle. Three times the M's sent me back to Tacoma. Each demotion chipped away at me. The last time, in mid-August, I sat at my Seattle locker with my head down, in tears. I felt drained, defeated.

"Come on, relax, you're going to get through this," teammates said.

Hurt and angry, I seriously thought about driving back to Miami. Instead, I called Mom.

"Forget them. I hate them all. I don't want to be here. I'm coming home," I said.

"No you're not!" Mom answered. "You don't have a house here if you come home. You have to stay out there. You are GOING TO MAKE IT!"

Allsport

Tom Dipace

Mike Urban/Seattle Post-Intelligencer

Wanting to quit during tough times is natural. There are times you should quit and try something else. But quitting out of frustration is rarely the right time. I'm so thankful Mom talked me out of it. I know now the adversity made me stronger.

If I had quit, I would have missed the Mariners' remarkable "Refuse To Lose" playoff run. In August, Seattle trailed California by 13 games. A magical string of victories closed the gap as I rejoined the team August 31st.

The playoff race excited me as much as the guys playing.

I saw it as a learning experience. I prepared myself each day to play. I paid attention to every detail, as if my life depended on it.

The season ended with us tied with California. We won the one-game playoff in dramatic fashion for the M's first-ever playoff spot.

I hit three times in the hard-fought playoff series against New York. What a thrill! What I'll remember most, though, is being on-deck in the roaring Kingdome when Edgar drove home Junior in the 11th inning to beat New York 6-5 in the deciding division playoff game. That's the best feeling I've had in baseball. There's nothing like winning.

The same could be said for losing.

Cleveland dashed our World Series visions 4-2 in the American League Championship Series.

With the season-ending loss at the

![Tacoma Rainiers]

Tacoma Rainiers

Above, I get caught in the celebration pig pile with Junior after beating New York. Below, I comfort Joey Cora after our amazing season ended. I told Joey how proud I was of him and the way he played. "Next year, it's going to be you and me, and we're going to win it all!" I said.

Robin Layton/Seattle Post-Intelligencer

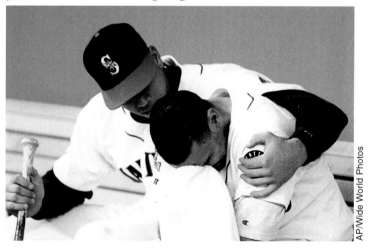

AP/Wide World Photos

Kingdome, Seattle fans gave us a thunderous, moving ovation after the game to show their thanks for the season's incredible ride that saved baseball in Seattle.

My prediction of winning it all didn't come true in 1996. We didn't even make the playoffs, thanks to untimely injuries to ace pitcher Randy Johnson and Griffey.

kept me in Seattle.

I made the All-Star team as the league's leading hitter. The honor overwhelmed me. Everything happened so fast that the whole All-Star weekend became a blur.

Seattle's four All-Stars in 1996, Dan Wilson, Jay Buhner, Edgar Martinez and Alex. Ken Griffey, Jr. and Randy Johnson were both injured.

My first full season in the majors still produced some great memories and made me feel I belonged in the big leagues.

I began the season wondering how many times I'd be sent down to Tacoma, especially after hitting .105 in my first 19 at-bats. A hot hitting streak that lasted most of the season

The numbers I put up that year were beyond my wildest goals.

After the season, my peers voted me Major League Player of the Year by a landslide, but baseball writers voted me second to Ranger Juan Gonzalez for the Most Valuable Player award. The 3-point margin was

One of my faults is a tendency to be late. One day I missed batting practice, BP as we call it. Randy and Jay cornered me and drilled me. "Who do you think you are?" they said. "I don't think I'm anyone. I'm sorry. I'll come early tomorrow." "You think you get a couple of hits and you don't need BP?" They both went on to say how much harder they work now than ever before. I wasn't angry with them. I knew they were just impressing a point.

Alex's 1996 stats

Batting average	358*
Runs scored	141*
Doubles	54*
Total bases	379*
Grand slams	3*
Home runs	36
RBIs	123

* League leader
Alex's batting average led both leagues and was the highest by a right-hander in 57 years.

Allsport

Tom Dipace

the closest in 36 years.

Yes, it hurt barely missing the prestigious award. But being bitter won't make it better. There will

always be deserved recognition you don't receive. That's part of life. I can't change the past, so I don't worry about it.

The 1997 season brought pride and disappointment. Nagging injuries dogged me throughout the season. I didn't post the numbers I did in 1996, but I still had a solid year, hitting .300.

Early in the season we were playing at Boston. We led going into the bottom of the ninth and should have won. But I made a throwing error that would have been the last out, and the Red Sox beat us in extra innings. I'm not proud of the error. I'm proud of how I reacted. My next at-bat, I doubled. That showed I didn't give up.

After the game, I stood tall and answered every reporter's question, basically admitting I messed up and couldn't wait to get out there tomorrow. I gained a measure of respect that day.

But I lost a little pride in myself later in the season when I threw a bat out of frustration. Thankfully it didn't hit anyone.

That night, Eddy, from the Boys Club, saw it on TV and called to scold me. He always tells me the truth, even if it hurts. He re-minded me that my actions can shame all those who helped me get this far—my family, friends, Eddy, Coach Hofman, and even Mr. Arteaga.

Nobody can act perfectly all the time. No doubt I'll make mistakes in the future. The thing is, we must always strive to do the right thing.

In my case, that means playing hard and honorably. In doing so, I honor all those people who have supported me throughout my life.

Tacoma Rainiers/Michael Sage

After winning the American League West title in 1997, it was ironic that we faced the Baltimore Orioles in the playoffs.

My first full-time playoff experience came against my longtime hero, Cal Ripken, Jr.

I first met Cal during spring training in Florida while I was still in high school. We met before a game and talked a few minutes. The thing that blew me away was he knew my name. He had read about me in the newspapers. I couldn't believe it.

"Cal Ripken knows my name!" I blurted to my family when I got home.

During the past four years I've gotten to know Cal as a personal friend. We've had many long talks, and he has given me sound advice.

"Work hard and respect the game," are the two most important things he has taught me. No question Cal has done both.

I've been to his home and seen his off-season workouts. Cal has to be the hardest working guy in sports. He loves to sweat. To compile his streak of playing for 15 years (and counting) without missing a game is unbelievable.

Cal also encourages me to keep learning. He's an avid book reader, and I try to be, too.

I also try to be on good terms with all my team-mates. I consider them all my friends. But the player I'm closest to is New York Yankee shortstop Derek Jeter.

We met as rookies and hit it off within five min-utes. We have so much in common it's like looking in the mirror. We talk all the time and have developed a tight bond.

We spend time together

"I love Alex like a brother. We have a good time together. We both work hard. We both understand we're blessed by the opportunities we have, and we try to be good people."
—Derek Jeter

"Alex's composure and maturity level are impressive. A lot of players come in with raw talent, but they don't know how to play or handle themselves off the field. Alex does both well."—Cal Ripken, Jr.

during and after the season. When I play in New York, I stay at his house, and he stays at mine when his team plays in Seattle.

What's special is we support each other through good times and bad. We can talk out our unique frustrations with each other.

Derek has a great work ethic, and being around him inspires me. Having a friend like that is more valuable than gold.

John McDonough/Sports Illustrated

Rod Mar/Seattle Times

Although being a million-aire at age 18 changed my material value, it hasn't changed my personal values.

San Francisco Giants star Barry Bonds once said to me, "Alex, the money doesn't make the man. The man makes the money."

I try to remember that. It's not how much you make that counts. It's what you do with it.

There's a popular song out with a line that says: "It's all about the Benjamins, baby." The Benjamins are $100 bills, which feature Benjamin Franklin's face.

So is life all about the money?

Not for me. Money allows me to travel, to learn first hand from experts, and to meet interesting people. But at the end of the day it doesn't make me feel better inside.

One thing that does make me feel better is using money in a positive way.

Not long after I became a professional, I started a scholarship fund at Westminster to give others the opportunity I had.

After the 1996 season, I decided to help rebuild the Miami Boys Club baseball field with a donation of $25,000.

Returning to my baseball roots brought back many memories. For a kid who couldn't afford a soda, handing that check to Eddy and throwing out the first pitch felt right and good.

Speaking at schools has shown me that sometimes encouragement is the best gift, and that doesn't cost anything.

I remember once fielding questions

Rod Mar/Seattle Tim

from kids at a Seattle school. A boy raised his hand and said, "Can I have a hug?"

I walked over and wrapped my arms around him. It was a special moment—a moment all the Benjamins in the world couldn't buy. So, you see, it's not all about the Benjamins.

"Setbacks and tribulations never stopped Alex from pursuing his dream. It didn't matter what happened around us, he was always focused on his goal."
—Lourdes, mother

"The thing about Alex is he worked hard for what he's achieved. Even while watching TV at home, he would lift weights."
—Susy, sister

"When Alex was little, all he wanted me to do was throw him Whiffle balls that he'd hit with a plastic bat. He had that drive from the beginning."
—Joe, brother

"Alex has changed my life. He made me realize the importance of my work at the Boys and Girls Clubs. Nobody has given back like Alex."
—Eddy Rodriguez

There are times when it seems all baseball is about is the autograph. So many people want it—it can be frightening. I could sign for 1,000 people, but the one person who didn't get an autograph might think I'm a jerk.

I remind myself that fame is fleeting. As funny as it sounds, my philosophy is to act and think like I have played my last baseball game.

I've seen a lot of players act confident and arrogant in the middle of their careers. As they go downhill, they become nicer, humbled by their decreased performance. By the time they retire, they're great citizens again. I want to be at that last level now.

If an injury suddenly ends my career tomorrow, I want people to like me for what I have inside.

That's not to say I'm complacent about my career. I want to improve myself on and off the field every year. I want to win world championships. This drive has always been inside me.

Still, all work and no play is not good either.

Alex hasn't changed as a person. People say Alex so lucky to have money and fame. I tell them he's ot lucky. He worked for it. He's e hardest working guy I know. henever we end a phone conrsation, he never says goode. He says, 'Keep working ard.'"
J.D. Arteaga, University of iami's all-time winningest cher, now with the Mets.

University of Miami Sports
Information Department

"What you see is what you get with Alex. Money hasn't changed him. There's no dark side to him. He gives back to a lot of people. He's the one who encouraged me to get back into baseball.
—James Colzie, former Florida State cornerback, now with the Montreal Expos.

"Alex is eager to learn and improve himself. In restaurants, sometimes we'll play word games on napkins or give each other spelling tests."
—Christina Centeno, Nike athlete marketing manager, who speaks three languages and works with Alex almost daily on off-field projects.

People always ask what I enjoy doing in my spare time. I enjoy going out with friends and meeting new people. I love to golf and play basketball whenever possible.

On the road I read a lot. And you might not believe this, but one thing I do when our team travels is visit various college campuses, just to be inspired. My continuing education is so important to me that in January of 1998 I took my first college courses. I'm determined to get a college degree some day. I don't care if it takes me 10 years.

As for this year, let's make a deal. Let's all hit a grand slam.